All the Dear
Little Animals

All the Dear Little Animals

Written by Ulf Nilsson
Illustrations by Eva Eriksson

Translated by Julia Marshall

GECKO PRESS

One day we had nothing to do.
We wanted some fun. Then Esther
found a bumblebee.

"Oh, here's something," she said,
"something sad and tragic."

The bee was furry, stripey—and dead.
She stroked it in her hand. Its wings were
tattered and its legs stuck out.

"Little bee," said Esther, her voice choked
with emotion. "I love you."

Esther was brave. I was just little. I was afraid of everything, especially of dying. I didn't even know anyone who'd died.

"You hold it," said Esther, "while I dig it a little grave."

I hid my hands.

"You're scared," she said, rolling her eyes.

"Bees can sting," I answered.

"It's dead, stupid," said Esther.

"I can write things," I said. "I can write a poem about how horrible death is."

She harrumphed and went to get a spade, some seeds that would grow into blue flowers, and a cigar box for a coffin.

We took the secret path to the secret clearing.

There Esther dug a deep hole and I wrote.
I'm a good writer because I think a lot and
there are lots of words inside me.

"Huh! Poems!" said Esther. She sweated,
and the sun shone, and birds sang in the
bushes.

We buried the bumblebee in the black hole.
We planted our seeds. We made a circle of
red and yellow flowers.

A dear little life in the hand
Suddenly gone, deep in the sand.

Esther wiped her nose. "Poor little bee,"
she said. "But life must go on."

She walked across the clearing and back. She had an idea coming.

"The world is full of dead things," she said. "In every bush there's a bird or a butterfly or a mouse. Someone has to look after them. Someone unselfish must make sure all these dead things get buried."

"Who must?" I asked.

"We must," she said.

We looked in bushes, under trees, and out in the fields, but there weren't many dead things around.

Esther's little brother Puttie helped, but we didn't tell him what we were looking for, so he didn't find anything. But he was so small it didn't matter.

At last we found a dead mouse.

"There!" Esther was pleased. "Now we have work to do."

"What's it doing, lying there?" asked Puttie.

"It's dead," said Esther.

"Why is it lying down?" Puttie asked.

We explained that every living thing must die—that even we will die one day and disappear. We told him how sad and sorrowful that is, and how everyone cries. At last Puttie understood.

"Me?" he said. "Will I die?"

"Not yet, silly boy," said Esther. "When you're an old man."

His lip started to tremble. He said, "But Mummy and Daddy will be so sad..."

"Hold the mouse!"

Esther gave me a funny smile.

I put my hands in my pockets and shook my head.

"I knew it! You're too scared to touch anything dead. Honestly!"

We showed Puttie the secret path and we all buried our little mouse friend.

Esther dug a grave in the middle of the clearing. She'd found another cigar box in the toolshed, and she nailed a cross together.

I read my poem.

Death lasts a thousand, thousand years.
Does it hurt to be dead?
Is it lonely? Is it frightening?

Puttie cried big fat tears. "Me too?"
he sniffed. "But Mummy will be so sad..."

We were very kind and good, looking
after the dead animals. We were the nicest
people in the world.

We had a lot of fun that boring summer day. We started a business called Funerals Ltd. We would hold the world's best funerals, and help all the poor dead animals on earth.

Esther's job was to dig. I would write the poems. And Puttie would cry.

We packed a suitcase with all the things
we'd need:

Shovel

Ice cream sticks for small crosses

Big sticks for big crosses

Hammer

Nails

Boxes—small and large—for coffins

Beautiful gravestones

Paintbrushes and paint

Seeds for blue flowers

Flowers—red and yellow

Esther phoned everyone who lived nearby.
I heard her on the phone. In the next village
she found a dead hamster named Harold.

"Fantastic! We'll bury Harold in the nicest possible way. Yes, the funeral can be at three. Yes, we can have lots of hymns! It's only five dollars, I mean ten. How long will we take care of the grave? For eternity. In a lovely clearing which won't ever be disturbed. Eternity it will be then. Great, lovely, right you are..."

Little Harold looked so sweet with his eyes closed.

"He might just be asleep," said Puttie, who wanted to wake him. "Hello!"

Esther said in her funeral voice: "He will sleep now for eternity. But we will never forget him. That's what we're paid for! You must be happy and kind to do this work, Puttie."

I got a stomachache. We had promised to
look after Harold's grave for eternity.

I wrote Harold-hymns—for singing very,
very slowly.

As winter comes down and it gets cold,
Farewell Harold, wee Harold so bold.
La la lu la, farewell, farewell.

The sun shone and it was warm. The girl who owned Harold cried and cried.

Puttie tried to make her feel better. He said, "If Harold gets better, we'll dig him up again. That's what we'll do, tra la lu."

He was painting the gravestone and humming.

Esther's father had a rooster for us to bury. It had grown old and tired.

The hens followed us down the secret path. Esther dug a big hole and we put the rooster in the grave, tucking in its tail.

Death comes just as the clock strikes ten.
Why? Why? Why just then?

We invited the hens to join the sad occasion, but they just pecked in the dirt for grubs.

"What's the matter with you chooks?" shouted Esther. "You have to be a little bit sad, you silly hens!"

Esther found three dead fish in a bag in the fridge.

"I like painting stones," said Puttie.

Here's one more fish,
Little fish in a dish.
Life is not always
Quite what you wish.

"You have to have a proper name," said
Esther. "You can't put 'here's one more fish'
on the gravestone, for heaven's sakes."

Grandma gave us nine mice from her mousetraps. Usually she fed them to the cat.

They had to have names, so first we had to baptize them. "I name you Paula Antonia. And you, Simon James." There was one very fat mouse.

Gretel the Great, we say good bye,
Take good care now, where you lie.

The clearing was starting to look like
a beautiful cemetery. But no one paid
us for the funerals.

Esther suddenly got cross. "It's a stupid funeral business! We only do small stuff and pointless animals. Soon we'll be collecting dead flies from windowsills. Or ants from down there in the gravel."

"These ones are running," said Puttie. "They're alive."

"Who cares. We can bury them anyway. They'll soon die."

Esther was very cross.

"I'd like to get a huge animal, a fat wild pig." Now she was daydreaming. "A big, fat, angry pig. So angry its heart exploded."

I made a rhyme:

A pig, a cow, a toad,
All no longer on life's road.

"Road?" Puttie was suddenly awake. "Squashed? Boomph!"

Squashed animals! Now Esther was happy again. We dragged our heavy funeral bag, full of crosses and stones, down the main road.

We found a flat hedgehog with a thousand
prickles. We had motorcycle gloves from
Esther's dad. We lay the hedgehog in the
grave. It was like a big flat loaf of bread.

In heaven you'll run with nice soft paws,
Not round in circles on squashed claws.

We looked on the road again. At last we
found something massive.

"This must be the longest hare in
Sweden!"

Esther danced around it.

"Since you think dead animals are yucky,"
she told me, "you can use the gloves."

Esther arranged the suitcase as a coffin.
We baptized the hare Ferdinand Axelson.
We made him very comfortable with a
pillow and a checked blanket.

"Now you are ready for your everlasting
journey!" said Esther.

Puttie cried. "What about me? Do I get a pillow when I die?"

"Yes, you'll get a pillow," said Esther.

"And my blankie?"

"Yes, your blankie, too."

"My rabbit?"

"Poor rabbit. How about your bear instead?"

"Food for me?"

"You'll have cakes and buns and juice if you want."

"All right," said Puttie, and he stopped crying.

Esther wiped his nose.

Rest in peace, rest while you may.
We'll see you soon, another day.

After my poem, Esther had tears in her
eyes. "Read that again," she said quietly.
"You write quite good poems, actually."

It began to get dark. We'd had such a good day. We'd been so kind. Now we were tired.

Two blackbirds went chasing through the trees. One of them hit the verandah window. Bang. I had never seen anything die. We crouched beside the blackbird. It fluttered. It opened its beak. Its leg shuddered. It only took a minute, then it was dead.

"Must bury it," said Puttie.

"Little blackbird, you'll get the best funeral in the world," said Esther.

"Yes, you'll be happy again," said Puttie.

I forgot to be scared. The blackbird was
so black it was shiny. It had a yellow beak.
When I picked it up it was very light.
I carried it into the clearing.

Esther didn't say anything.

"It might have babies," said Puttie.
"And a mother."

"We'll call him Little One," I said.

We prepared the grave. We lit a candle and we wrote "Little One" on our most beautiful stone. I held Little One and read out my poem.

Your song is finished. Life is gone.
Your warm body grows cold and it's
        getting dark.
In the darkness you shine like a star.
Thank you for being alive!

Another blackbird sang a beautiful song.
got a frog in my throat when I read.
Esther cried. We all felt very reverent.
Sadness lay like a black
quilt over the clearing.
And Puttie went to sleep.

Life is long and death is short
It takes but a minute to die.
Yet up will grow the grass
Moss and flowers will bloom
And stillness will come at last...

The next day we found something else to do. Something completely different.

This edition first published in 2020 by Gecko Press
PO Box 9335, Wellington 6141, New Zealand
info@geckopress.com

English-language edition © Gecko Press Ltd 2020
Translation © Julia Marshall 2006

First published by Bonnier Carlsen Bokförlaget, Stockholm, Sweden
Published in the English language by arrangement with Bonnier Carlsen
Bokförlaget, Stockholm, Sweden

First English-language edition published by Gecko Press 2006

Distributed in the United States and Canada by Lerner Publishing Group
lernerbooks.com
Distributed in the United Kingdom by Bounce Sales and Marketing
bouncemarketing.co.uk
Distributed in Australia and New Zealand by Walker Books Australia
walkerbooks.com.au

Editing and poems by Penelope Todd
Design and typesetting by Esther Chua
Handwriting by Giselle Clarkson
Printed in China by Everbest Printing Co. Ltd, an accredited
ISO 14001 & FSC-certified printer

ISBN hardback (USA) 978-1-776572-89-2
ISBN paperback 978-1-776572-82-3
Ebook available
Previous editions: 978-0-958259-89-7; 978-0-958259-88-0

For more curiously good books, visit geckopress.com